ANIMAL VS. ANIMAL

WHO'S THE

# BIGGEST?

BY EMILIE DUFRESNE

Gareth Stevens
PUBLISHING

Please visit our website, www.garethstevens.com. For a free color catalog of all our high-quality books, call toll free 1-800-542-2595 or fax 1-877-542-2596.

Cataloging-in-Publication Data

Names: Dufresne, Emilie.
Title: Who's the biggest? / Emilie Dufresne.
Description: New York: Gareth Stevens Publishing, 2022. | Series: Animal vs. animal | Includes glossary and index.
Identifiers: ISBN 9781534537347 (pbk.) | ISBN 9781534537361 (library bound) | ISBN 9781534537354 (6 pack) | ISBN 9781534537378 (ebook)
Subjects: LCSH: Body size--Juvenile literature. | Animals--Juvenile literature.
Classification: LCC QL799.3 D843 2022 | DDC 591.4'1--dc23

Published in 2022 by
**Gareth Stevens Publishing**
29 East 21st Street
New York, NY 10010

Edited by: Holly Duhig
Designed by: Danielle Rippengill

CPSIA compliance information: Batch #CSGS22: For further information contact Gareth Stevens, New York, New York at 1-800-542-2595.

Find us on

# IMAGE CREDITS

# CONTENTS

Words that look like this can be found in the glossary on page 24.

# THE GREAT AND SMALL GAMES

### Step right up!
It's the Great and Small Games!
See nature's biggest and heaviest creatures in action!

### Today's events:
**The Weigh-In!**
**The Hoopla!**
**The Dunk Tank!**

These events will surely decide once and for all:
Who's the Biggest?

Welcome, welcome, one and all,
to games where creatures GREAT and SMALL
have come to show off their size and girth
and **prove** they are the biggest on Earth.
With MIGHTY MONSTERS and gentle giants,
it's time to see which one will **triumph**.
So let me, Ringo, take you to see
the CHALLENGES, of which there are three...

# THE CONTENDERS

Let's find out some facts and figures about today's contenders!

**Polar Bear**
The Ice Giant

**Size:** Up to 10 feet (3 m)

**Lives:** Arctic

**Big Boast:**
Biggest **species** of bear

**African Elephant**
Wide Load

**Size:** 13 feet (4 m) tall

**Lives:** Sub-Saharan Africa

**Big Boast:**
Largest land **mammal**

**Giraffe**
The Savanna Skyscraper

**Size:** Up to 19 feet (5.8 m) tall

**Lives:** Sub-Saharan Africa

**Big Boast:**
The land mammal with the longest neck

**Colossal Squid**
The Tentacled Titan

**Size:** 33 feet (10 m) long

**Lives:** Oceans worldwide

**Big Boast:**
As long as a bus

**Lion's Mane Jellyfish**
Super Squish

**Size:** 100 feet (30 m) with tentacles

**Lives:** Arctic Sea, northern Atlantic and Pacific Oceans

**Big Boast:**
Largest species of jellyfish

**Blue Whale**
The Monster Mouth

**Size:** 105 feet (32 m) long

**Lives:** Oceans worldwide

**Big Boast:** Its heart can be as big as a car

# POLAR BEAR

GRAHH!

Rrrrrrround Onnnne!

The biggest bear on Earth may look cuddly, but don't let that fool you. The Ice Giant is the biggest **carnivore** on the planet. He's hidden by his snowy-colored **camouflage**, but he's large and he's in charge!

**Nickname:**
The Ice Giant

**Big Bonus:**
With paws the size of a dinner plate, this big bear is a surprisingly speedy swimmer, and can swim at 6 miles (10 km) per hour!

# VS. GIRAFFE

The Savanna Skyscraper holds his claim to fame as the longest-necked land mammal and can grow as tall as three humans standing on top of each other!

**Nickname:**
The Savanna Skyscraper

**Big Bonus:**
This hungry **herbivore** needs a lot of food to keep him going. Giraffes can eat around 100 pounds (45 kg) of twigs and leaves a day!

It's not only their necks that are long; their tongues can grow to a sticky 21 inches (53 cm) long!

# THE WEIGH-IN

Contenders, it's time to see once and for all which of you is the biggest. The first one to ring the bell at the top of the weighing scales will win the round!

1500 lbs

Polar bears have a layer of **blubber** that can be up to 4 inches (10 cm) thick!

**Polar Bear**

**Weight:** 1,500 pounds (680 kg)

The Ice Giant is impressive, but is it enough to beat the giraffe? The Savanna Skyscraper must be packing some weight in that neck! The bell is ringing and the contest is over!

Giraffe

Weight: 2,800 pounds (1,270 kg)

2800 lbs

A male giraffe can weigh around 2,800 pounds (1,270 kg). That's one big animal!

Round one goes to the **giraffe!**

# COLOSSAL SQUID VS.

**Rrrrrrround Twoooo!**

**SWOOSH**

This mysterious monster lives in the depths of the ocean, and though scientists don't know much about this immense **invertebrate**, they do know that it is big – really big!

**Nickname:**
The Tentacled Titan

**Big Bonus:**
This Tentacled Titan has three hearts to pump blood around its huge body!

# LION'S MANE JELLYFISH

This super squishy sea creature is the largest jellyfish in the ocean. It can grow tentacles that are longer than a blue whale!

**Nickname:**
Super Squish

**Big Bonus:**
This jiggly jellyfish may look large, but 95% of it is actually water!

The lion's mane jellyfish is bioluminescent (say: by-oh-lume-in-ess-ent), which means that it glows in the dark!

SWISH SWOOSH

# THE HOOPLA

It's time to see which of these super sea creatures is the widest! The hoop will be thrown over their heads, and whoever's hoop falls farthest down their body loses!

The colossal squid's mantle is nearly 40 inches (102 cm) wide!

# AFRICAN ELEPHANT

**Rrrrrrround Threee!**

**TOOT! TOOT!**

The African elephant is the largest land mammal on Earth. Weighing in at over 15,400 pounds (6,985 kg) and with a foot that is 20 inches (50.8 cm) wide, this massive mammal is feeling confident.

**Nickname:**
Wide Load

**Big Bonus:**
Even this mammal's molars are big; each one weighs 9 pounds (4 kg)!

# VS. BLUE WHALE

The blue whale is the biggest animal ever to have lived on Earth. That's right – this oversized ocean diver is bigger than even the dinosaurs!

**Nickname:**
The Arctic Avenger

**Big Bonus:**
Even baby blue whales are big. A blue whale calf is born weighing 4.4 tons (4 tonnes) and can gain 200 pounds (90 kg) a day!

★

Whales can eat up to 4 million <u>krill</u> in a day

WAONGH!

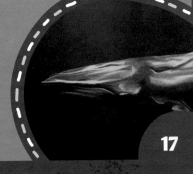

# THE DUNK TANK

These two contenders are now going face to face to see which can make the biggest splash! The African elephant only makes a small splash!

The contender with the biggest <u>surface area</u> and weight will push the most water out of the pool and make the biggest splash.

18

# HALL OF FAME

## Ostrich
The world's largest bird.

**Lives:** African savanna

**Eats:** Plants, seeds, insects, and lizards

**Size:** 9 feet (2.8 m) tall, 350 pounds (158 kg)

## Narwhal
Has a very long horn.

**Lives:** Arctic Sea

**Eats:** Fish, squid, and shrimp

**Size:** 20 feet (6 m) long including horn

## Wandering Albatross
Largest wingspan of any bird.

**Lives:** Antarctic region

**Eats:** Small fish and <u>crustaceans</u>

**Size:** Wings are 11.5 feet (3.5 m) across

## Saltwater Crocodile
World's largest crocodile.

**Lives:** Eastern India, Southeast Asia, and northern Australia

**Eats:** Any animal

**Size:** 16.5 feet (5 m) long

# QUIZ AND...

We've seen the animals big and tall,
now let's see if we know it all!

## Questions

1. What animal is the largest type of bear?

2. How tall is a giraffe?

3. What makes up 95% of the lion's mane jellyfish?

4. How much weight can a baby blue whale put on in a day?

5. What type of bird has the largest wingspan?

6. What is the biggest bird on the planet?

# ...ACTIVITY

Yoga is a great exercise for stretching out and making you reach the tallest and widest you can possibly reach. Let's try some poses!

**Tree Pose**

**Headstand**

# GLOSSARY

| | |
|---|---|
| **blubber** | a thick layer of fat under the skin of sea mammals |
| **camouflage** | traits that allow an animal to hide itself in a habitat |
| carnivore | an animal that eats other animals rather than plants |
| **crustacean** | a type of animal that lives in water and has a hard outer shell |
| **herbivore** | an animal that only eats plants |
| invertebrate | an animal that does not have a backbone |
| **krill** | small crustaceans found in salt water that are classified as plankton |
| **mammal** | an animal that has warm blood, a backbone, and produces milk |
| mantle | the "head" part of a squid |
| **species** | a group of very similar animals or plants that are capable of producing more of their kind |
| **surface area** | how big the surface of an object is |

# INDEX